EVANSTON PUBLIC LIBRARY

9250

W9-DIP-047

JPicture Pinkw.D

Pinkwater, Daniel Manus,
 1941-
Tooth-Gnasher Superflash
 /
    1990, c198

TOOTH=GNASHER SUPERFLASH

by Daniel Pinkwater

EVANSTON PUBLIC LIBRARY
CHILDREN'S DEPARTMENT
1703 ORRINGTON AVENUE
EVANSTON, ILLINOIS 60201

Macmillan Publishing Company   New York
Collier Macmillan Publishers   London

Also by Daniel Pinkwater

Aunt Lulu
Guys from Space
Uncle Melvin
The Wuggie Norple Story

Copyright © 1981 by Daniel M. Pinkwater. All rights reserved. No part of this book may be reproduced or transmitted in any form or by any means, electronic or mechanical, including photocopying, recording, or by any information storage and retrieval system, without permission in writing from the Publisher. Macmillan Publishing Company, 866 Third Avenue, New York, NY 10022. Collier Macmillan Canada, Inc.   First Edition 1981; reissued 1990. Printed in the United States of America   10 9 8 7 6 5 4 3 2 1

Library of Congress Cataloging-in-Publication Data
Pinkwater, Daniel Manus, date.   Tooth-Gnasher Superflash / by Daniel Pinkwater.   p.   cm.   Summary: The Popsnorkle family test drives the Tooth-Gnasher Superflash, pleased with the car's ability to turn into several different animals.   ISBN 0-02-774655-0   [1. Automobiles — Fiction.]   I. Title.   [PZ7.P6335To 1990] [E] — dc20
89-18207   CIP   AC

To Al,

who keeps the old green Thunderclap going

Mr. Popsnorkle decided it was time to buy a new car. His old car, a green Thunderclap-Eight, was just about worn out.

So Mr. Popsnorkle and Mrs. Popsnorkle and the five little Popsnorkles all got into the worn-out green Thunderclap-Eight and went looking for a nice new car.

They drove down to the highway where all the car dealers were and looked at all the signs and shiny new cars in the windows.

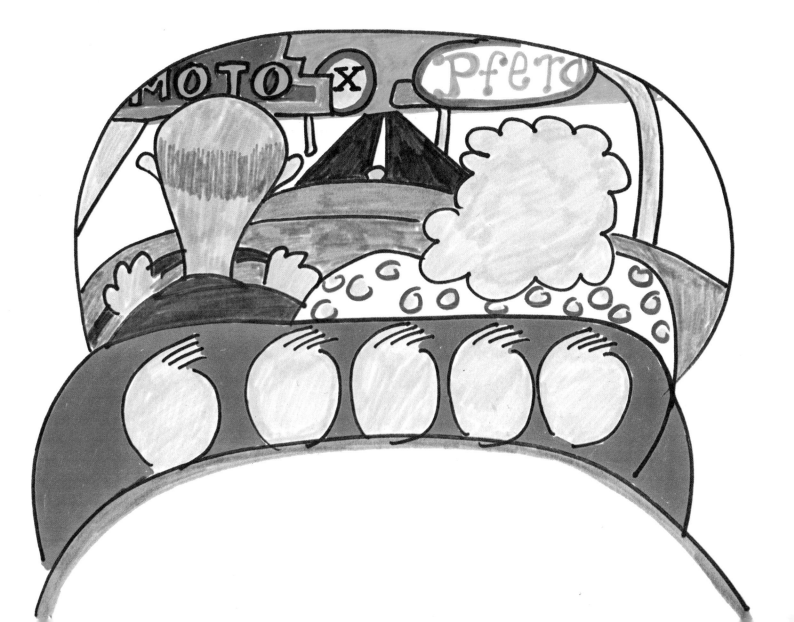

"Look!" shouted the five little Popsnorkles. "The Tooth-Gnasher Superflash! That's a great car!"

"It is a pretty color," said Mrs. Popsnorkle. (It was light blue.)

Mr. Popsnorkle turned into the parking lot of the Tooth-Gnasher car dealer. A salesman came out. "I am Mr. Sandy," said the car salesman. "May I show you the new Tooth-Gnasher Superflash? We only have one left."

"Is it the light-blue one?" Mrs. Popsnorkle asked.

Mr. Popsnorkle and Mrs. Popsnorkle and the five little Popsnorkles and Mr. Sandy, the car salesman, all got into the Tooth-Gnasher Superflash. Mr. Sandy drove, and Mr. Popsnorkle sat next to him. Mrs. Popsnorkle and the five little Popsnorkles all sat in the back seat.

"See how smooth it rides?" Mr. Sandy asked.

"We love this car!" shouted the five little Popsnorkles. "Buy it, Daddy!"

"It is a beautiful light blue," Mrs. Popsnorkle said.

"Would it be all right if I drove the car for a while?" Mr. Popsnorkle asked Mr. Sandy, the car salesman. Mr. Sandy pulled over to the side of the road and got out and opened the door for Mrs. Popsnorkle, who got in the front seat with Mr. Popsnorkle, who had moved over behind the steering wheel. Mr. Sandy, the car salesman, got in the back seat with the five little Popsnorkles.

"Yaay!" shouted the five little Popsnorkles. "Daddy is going to drive the Tooth-Gnasher Superflash!"

Mr. Popsnorkle started the Tooth-Gnasher Superflash. It roared out onto the highway. The tires squealed. Other drivers honked their horns.

"Yaay!" the five little Popsnorkles shouted.

"Perhaps you shouldn't drive quite so fast until you are used to the car," Mr. Sandy, the car salesman, said.

"What does this button do?" Mr. Popsnorkle asked as he pushed a button on the dashboard. The Tooth-Gnasher Superflash rose up on its rear wheels and zoomed along the highway with its nose high in the air.

"This is very nice," Mr. Popsnorkle said. "And what does this button do?" He pushed another button, and the car began to rock from side to side on its rear wheels. Then the rear wheels turned into little legs — and the car turned into a dinosaur, running on its hind legs.

"Fine," said Mr. Popsnorkle. "I like a car that turns into a dinosaur. And what does this button do?" He pushed another button.

The dinosaur put his nose down near the road and began to run on all fours. Then the Tooth-Gnasher Superflash turned into a galloping elephant.

"Yaay!" the five little Popsnorkles shouted.

"It turns into an elephant, too, dear." Mr. Popsnorkle said to Mrs. Popsnorkle.

"That's very nice, dear," said Mrs. Popsnorkle, "and such a lovely color — but do you have to go so fast?"

"Of course not," Mr. Popsnorkle said. "Now let's see what this button does." He pushed another button, and the Tooth-Gnasher Superflash changed from a galloping elephant to a gigantic turtle.

"My goodness, this is really a good car," Mr. Popsnorkle said. "It turns into a dinosaur and an elephant and a turtle. Can it do anything else?"

"I really don't know," said Mr. Sandy, the car salesman. "I've never had a car turn into a dinosaur or an elephant or a turtle before. This is not the way the Tooth-Gnasher Super-flash is supposed to behave."

"Well, it's just the way I think a car should behave," said Mr. Popsnorkle. "The only thing I'd like this car to do besides turning into a dinosaur and an elephant and a gigantic turtle would be to turn into a huge chicken and fly. Now let's see if there's a button that will do that." Mr. Popsnorkle found another button on the dashboard and pushed it.

The Tooth-Gnasher Superflash turned into a huge chicken and flew all the way back to the car dealer's.

"This is a first-class car," Mr. Popsnorkle said. "We'll take it."

"Yaay!" shouted the five little Popsnorkles.

"It certainly is a lovely color," said Mrs. Popsnorkle

"I never saw a car do any of those things," said Mr. Sandy, the car salesman.

Mr. Popsnorkle and Mrs. Popsnorkle and the five little Popsnorkles traded in their worn-out green Thunderclap-Eight and gave Mr. Sandy lots of money. They drove away in their new light-blue Tooth-Gnasher Superflash.

"Yaay! We love our new car!" the five little Popsnorkles shouted.

"It really *is* a lovely color," said Mrs. Popsnorkle.

"It's a nice car all right," said Mr. Popsnorkle. "But it can't do half the things our good old Thunderclap-Eight could do."